Bantam Books in the Choose Your Own Adventure® Series
Ask your bookseller for the books you have missed

THE MAGIC OF THE UNICORN

BY DEBORAH LERME GOODMAN

ILLUSTRATED BY RON WING

An R.A. Montgomery Book

BANTAM BOOKS

TORONTO • NEW YORK • LONDON • SYDNEY • AUCKLAND

RL 5, IL age 10 and up

THE MAGIC OF THE UNICORN
A Bantam Book / December 1985

CHOOSE YOUR OWN ADVENTURE® is a registered trademark of
Bantam Books, Inc. Registered in U.S. Patent and Trademark
Office and elsewhere.

Original conception of Edward Packard.

ISBN 0-553-25242-9

Published simultaneously in the United States and Canada

Bantam Books are published by Bantam Books, Inc. Its trademark, consisting of the words "Bantam Books" and the por-
trayal of a rooster, is Registered in U.S. Patent and Trademark
Office and in other countries. Marca Registrada. Bantam
Books, Inc., 666 Fifth Avenue, New York, New York 10103.

PRINTED IN THE UNITED STATES OF AMERICA

O   0 9 8 7 6 5 4 3

To John, with thanks for your magic

WARNING!!!

Do not read this book straight through from beginning to end! It contains many different adventures you may have as you search for a unicorn. From time to time as you read along, you will be asked to make a choice. Your choice may lead to success or disaster.

Only you are responsible for your fate because only you can make these decisions. After you make each choice, follow the instructions to see what happens to you next.

Think carefully before you act. The magic of the unicorn is very powerful. Will you use it to save your village—or will you be trapped forever under an evil spell? You're about to find out.

Good luck!

The summer of 1507 is exceptionally dry throughout Flanders. Fires scorch the forests, crops wither, and animals collapse with thirst. Nowhere is the drought as severe as in your own small village. Just last week, when you went to check the dwindling water supply, you discovered a dead rat floating in the well upon which everyone depended. Since then the water has been foul and tainted. The barrels of rainwater are nearly empty, and all attempts to dig a new well have yielded nothing but dry earth.

One morning, after weeding the field you inherited when your parents died ten years ago, you pay a visit to Marie-Claire. She is the oldest person in the village and one of your special friends.

Turn to page 2.

"Some people say this might be the last summer any of us lives to see," you tell her sadly. "None of the other villages around has enough water to share with us. And it's hopeless to keep trying to dig a new well. I wish there were something I could do about it."

Marie-Claire looks up from her knitting. "You could try to lure a unicorn to the well. Why, the touch of its horn purifies even poison."

"But, Marie-Claire," you exclaim, "around here unicorns are rarer than water! I bet it would be easier to find the sorceress than a unicorn."

"That's a good idea!" she replies. "I'm sure the sorceress knows all about unicorns. Why don't you look for her?"

"But no one has seen her in years," you remind Marie-Claire. "The last person who tried to find her never even returned!"

"Ah, but you are ten times smarter than anyone who has ever searched for the sorceress. If anyone can find her, it is you."

Although you feel flattered, you are not sure you are really clever enough.

"Well, I'll give it a try. I wonder if I still remember that riddle describing the way to find the sorceress. Is this right?" You take a deep breath and recite:

> "Near a land reserved for woe,
> In a place that's high but low,
> Watch which way the bat doth go,
> Find me there, and I will know."

Turn to page 5.

You decide to climb to the top of the highest hill. Once there you wipe your brow and look around. Feeling a little perplexed, you remind yourself of the next line of the riddle: "Watch which way the bat doth go." But there are no bats in sight.

As you pace impatiently, wondering what to do, you come upon a cave opening near the top of the hill. You poke your head inside, but it is too dark to see anything. "Hello, hello!" you call, but only your own voice echoes back.

The cave seems like a perfect place to find a bat, and maybe even the sorceress as well.

If you enter the cave to look for the bat, turn to page 34.

If you think it best to watch for a bat before you do anything else, turn to page 27.

"Perfect!" says
Marie-Claire as she
hands you a glass pendant
shaped like a raindrop. "Put
on my good-luck talisman.
Use it as you need it, my friend."
You say good-bye to
Marie-Claire, then roam the
parched fields. After pondering the riddle,
you think of two places reserved for woe.
The sorceress could mean the village
graveyard or the small camp outside the village
where two lepers live in gloomy isolation.

If you head for the graveyard, turn to page 11.

*If you decide to go to the lepers' camp,
turn to page 8.*

6

Filled with horror, you race away from the villagers. You slowly realize you can't go home, but cling to the hope that their panic will subside in a few days—especially if you find a way to purify the well. Since you can't continue your search for the sorceress by investigating the graveyard, you decide to concentrate on finding a unicorn.

You turn away from your village and walk along the road toward the forest, hoping to find a unicorn there. Before long you hear a cart approaching behind you.

The driver is Simon, a traveling peddler you've always liked. You wave to him and ask, "Where are you going?"

Simon pulls the cart to a halt beside you. "Everyone around here is too upset about the drought to take much interest in my trinkets. I'm going to try my luck in the city of Arras. At least people will be trading there. Want to join me? I wouldn't mind some company for such a long trip."

Arras! You've never been to the city before. Although you would love to go, you suspect unicorns are more likely to live in the forest. But maybe you could meet someone in Arras who could tell you how to find a unicorn.

If you decide to search for a unicorn in the forest, turn to page 12.

If you climb in the cart headed for Arras, turn to page 14.

8

You turn down the path to the lepers' shabby hut. You know the villagers stay far from the lepers for fear of catching their dreaded skin disease, and they will be very upset if they ever learn you visited the lepers. When you first glimpse the two swollen faces peering out the doorway, you panic, then force yourself to continue toward them.

"Welcome, friend. Please come inside," says one of the lepers warmly.

"Thanks, but I'll stay outside," you reply. "I'm looking for the sorceress. The riddle says she lives near a place of woe, and I thought that might mean your home."

"Since no one will have anything to do with us, this is indeed a woeful place," says the second leper. "But I don't think it's the one your riddle describes. We have never seen the sorceress. In fact, I think even she must be afraid of catching our disease."

"Is leprosy that bad?" you ask.

"No," says the first man, "but the way people treat us is horrible. In fact, you'd better hurry back. If anyone sees you here, they won't let you return home."

Turn to page 19.

"Will you help me climb up the steeple?" you ask Brother Michel.

"I'll hoist you onto the rafter, but after that you're on your own," he says. "I'm afraid to climb that high."

Brother Michel lifts you over his head up toward the rafter. You grab the beam. After a few seconds of scrambling you right yourself safely on the rafter.

"What are you going to do next?" calls Brother Michel nervously.

You look around. "See that rope dangling from the church bell? Would you please move it closer so I can grab hold of it and climb all the way to the top of the steeple?"

He takes hold of the bottom of the rope and carries it toward you. "I can't bring it any closer," he says.

"I'll have to take a leap. Let's hope I can grab that rope!" you tell him with more confidence than you actually feel. "Here goes!"

Turn to page 23.

10

Emil smiles and slaps your back. "I'll teach you to be such a fine weaver that even the queen will buy your tapestries! Come on, let's find a messenger to carry the magic tapestry to your village."

Before long you are skillful enough to work on even the most elaborate tapestries. The days fly quickly, and at night, when you walk through the busy streets of Arras with your new friends from the studio, you often find yourself thinking how happy you are. But sometimes, just before you fall asleep, you think about your village. Since no one there can read or write, you aren't surprised that you haven't heard from anyone, but you can't help wondering if the magic tapestry really worked.

Turn to page 89.

Even though the path to the graveyard is all downhill, you are hot and thirsty by the time you arrive there. You sit in the shade of a drooping tree to cool off. As you watch parched leaves float to the dusty ground, you consider the next line of the riddle: "In a place that's high but low."

What can be both high and low? Looking around, you notice the rolling slopes of the hills along the far side of the graveyard. They seem to be both high and low. But then the churchbell rings, striking noon. Turning, you realize the steeple of the church also fits the riddle. The church itself is in a low valley, but the steeple towers high above the village.

If you walk over to the hills, turn to page 3.

If you enter the church, turn to page 16.

"Thanks, but I can't go with you now. How about another time?" you tell Simon. You wave good-bye as he continues down the road. When he disappears from view, you leave the road and make your way into the shadowy forest.

The air is parched and still; even the birds are quiet. As you travel deeper into the forest the only sound you hear is the crunching of your footsteps on dry leaves. After several hours of walking, you notice a few long strands of silver tangled in a bush. You hold your discovery up to the light, trying to decide whether it is fine thread or hair. You've never seen anything like it.

As you look around for other strands of silver, you spot several small hoofprints. They are too little to belong to a horse and aren't the right shape for a deer. Your heart stops for a second when you realize the hoofprints and the silver strands may be traces of a unicorn!

You search for more evidence and are surprised to see that the hoofprints lead in one direction and the silver hairs in another. You pause, trying to decide which way to go.

If you follow the hoofprints, turn to page 32.

If you head in the direction of the silver strands, turn to page 51.

14

For three days, while you ride through the forest on your way to Arras, you keep your eyes open for any sign of the unicorn. When you reach the outskirts of the city, you tell Simon about your search for a unicorn.

"It's a good thing you mentioned this," he says. "I happen to know that the Duchess of Arras has a unicorn horn. She keeps it on hand in case someone tries to poison her wine. I've heard she dips the horn in her goblet before she takes a sip. Maybe the Duchess will lend you her unicorn horn."

"That's a good idea," you answer, "but do you really think the Duchess would let me borrow it?"

"That's hard to say," Simon admits. "I've also heard there's a tapestry weaver in Arras who knows a lot about unicorn magic. He might be willing to help you."

If you decide to ask the Duchess to lend you her unicorn horn, turn to page 25.

If you ask Simon to take you to the weaver, turn to page 36.

You shudder with fear, but force yourself to crawl through the tunnel. The lantern casts eerie shadows on the webs. Spiders scurry under your shins. Strangely enough, you think you hear a faint sound of gurgling water.

Just then a bat swoops toward you. You flatten yourself to the ground and quickly cover your head with your hands. The bat soars over you, then flies straight through the wall of webs, creating a new tunnel.

You shine the light of the lantern into the bat's passageway, but all you can see is blackness. You'd like to follow the bat to see if it leads you to the sorceress, but you also want to find out what's making the gurgling noise.

If you decide to chase the bat, turn to page 76.

If you continue down the tunnel you are in now, turn to page 38.

When you go inside the church, Brother Michel looks up from the candelabrum he is polishing. "I was just wishing for some company. What are you up to, my friend?"

"I'm looking for the sorceress." You explain your interpretation of the riddle.

Brother Michel strokes his chin. "I don't believe anyone has ever considered the graveyard or steeple when figuring out that riddle, so you may be on the right track."

"The next line of the riddle says to watch which way the bat goes," you tell him. "Have you ever seen bats here?"

"Plenty!" he exclaims. "At night they fly around the steeple. I've heard them down in the cellar, too, although I never actually go there."

"I didn't know there was a cellar under the church."

"Oh, there's a crawl space there, but it's too small to be very useful," says Brother Michel. "Not only that, it's so infested with spiders that no one dares set foot in it. In fact, it would be a clever place for the sorceress to hide. If I had the courage, I'd look there."

Go on to the next page.

You are tempted to investigate the cellar, even though you don't like the idea of running into a web full of spiders. You also remind yourself that the riddle mentions a place that's high but low, and the cellar doesn't fit that description as well as the steeple does.

If you want to explore the cellar,
turn to page 20.

If you think the steeple is a better choice,
turn to page 9.

You say good-bye to the men and head toward home. As you reach the road to the village you meet several of your neighbors. Their faces whiten. Their eyes dart back and forth between you and the lepers, who are still standing by their doorway.

"Stay back!" shouts one man. "Keep away!"

"It's all right," you insist. "I was just there for a minute."

"You can't return to the village! Go back to the lepers!" shrieks another neighbor, eyeing you fearfully.

As you start to follow them the villagers gather stones. "Leper! Leper!" they scream, throwing rocks at you.

Turn to page 6.

"I'd like to explore the cellar," you tell Brother Michel.

He smiles at you and says, "Let me get you a lantern, then I'll show you the way." He leads you to a far corner of the church, where he opens a heavy trap door. "There are no stairs," he explains, "since the space is only about three feet high. You'll have to jump down and then crawl."

"Wish me luck!" you say as you lower yourself through the hole. When your feet reach the ground, Brother Michel hands you the lantern. You get down on your hands and knees, take a deep breath to calm yourself, and adjust the lantern. Only then do you see the spiders! Thousands, maybe millions of them are clustered on dense veils of cobwebs that fill the entire space except for a narrow passageway.

Turn to page 15.

You hurl your body toward the rope and miraculously manage to grab it tightly. As you sway from side to side the clanging of the bell is almost deafening.

"Oh, no!" wails Brother Michel. "Now the whole village will come running to find out why the bell is ringing. Just wait till they see I've allowed you to climb all over the church!"

You pay no attention. A trap door by the base of the bell has swung open, releasing a frightened bat. It flutters anxiously around you, then swoops out the window below.

"What's behind that door up there?" you ask Brother Michel.

"I had no idea it was there!" he replies.

Then the next line of the riddle—"Watch which way the bat doth go"—springs into your mind. You think you should probably follow the bat out the window, but you're very curious about the trap door.

If you begin climbing down to follow the bat, turn to page 50.

If you can't wait a minute longer to find out what's behind the trap door, turn to page 69.

The two of you make your way through the sun-streaked forest. Even though you know the unicorn has lost its horn, you feel certain you'll find a way to clean the well.

"Maybe the unicorn could tell me where to find another unicorn—one that still has its horn," you chatter happily. "I bet the unicorn must know all kinds of ways to clean water."

You soon reach a small clearing. There a crowd of woodland animals is gathered around the unicorn, who is lying on the ground.

"Oooh, no!" moans the owl.

"What's wrong?" you ask. "Is the unicorn sleeping? I don't mind waiting."

The animals turn to stare at you.

"You're too late," says a squirrel. "The unicorn is dead."

The End

"Let's see if the Duchess will let me borrow her unicorn horn," you tell Simon. "Besides, I'm curious. I've never met a duchess!"

The clamor of jostling carts and crowds of people startles you as you ride through the dry and dusty streets of Arras. You are still marveling at the strange sights and sounds when the cart stops in front of the most enormous building you have ever seen. You count *four* stories!

Simon helps you out of the cart. You march over to a guard standing solemnly by the front door and say, "I'd like to see the Duchess."

Turn to page 31.

Sweat streams down your face as you wait by the cave. At sunset you finally spot a bat zigzagging through the air. Instead of flying into the cave beside you, it soars to the side of the hill where you follow it into a second cave you haven't seen before.

You shiver with excitement as you grope your way through the darkness, listening to the sound of beating wings. Suddenly lightning streaks across your path, striking the ground just inches from your toes. Before you can catch your breath, a second bolt flashes, followed immediately by yet another.

Your heart is pounding with terror when you hear someone mutter, "Magic Mother of Merlin! Where's the thunder?"

"Who's there?" you call nervously.

Turn to page 33.

You are undaunted. "What about unicorns? Do you know anything about them?" you ask the sorceress. "I've heard they can purify water."

The words have barely left your lips when you see a handsome unicorn stepping lightly around the cave. You reach out to stroke its flank, but the unicorn vanishes abruptly.

"Just an illusion," the sorceress explains. "It's as close as I can come to creating a real unicorn, but it's no good for cleaning water."

"Have you ever seen a real unicorn?"

"Several times," she replies casually. "In fact, there's a unicorn living in the forest."

"Can you tell me where to find it in the forest?"

She shakes her head. "I'm afraid not, but I should be able to help you some other way. If you'll excuse me, I'm going to change into something more comfortable. I always think more clearly as the wind."

Go on to the next page.

You watch with astonishment as she flings her purple robe over her shoulder and spins until she seems to be a lavender tornado. The next thing you know, the tornado fades, and a cold wind rushes around the cave, howling and shrieking. A violet cloud slowly forms, and from it the sorceress emerges.

"I've got it!" she announces breathlessly. "I can cast one of two spells that may help you find the unicorn. I can give you the power to speak with animals, or I can knit you a golden net for catching magical beasts. Take your pick."

If you answer, "I want to be able to talk with animals," turn to page 44.

If you say, "Would you please make me the golden net?" turn to page 49.

He eyes your coarse clothing disdainfully and answers, "The Duchess is away."

"When will she return?"

The guard does not even look at you when he replies, "Not today."

"Tomorrow?"

He glances at you with impatience. "The Duchess alone decides when she will return."

"May I wait inside?"

"No." The guard points to a stone bench several yards from the door. "You may wait there."

You turn to Simon, not knowing what to do. "Shall I take you to the tapestry workshop? Maybe you'll have better luck there," he suggests.

You would like to see more of the city, and who knows how long the Duchess will be gone? Yet it may be worth waiting to ask her about her unicorn horn.

If you accept Simon's offer and climb back in the cart, turn to page 36.

If you say good-bye to Simon and wait for the Duchess, turn to page 35.

You track the hoofprints to a small clearing.
There you find a small white horse nibbling wild
flowers. The animal raises its head and stares at
you for a second before breaking into a frenzied
gallop. You hesitate, trying to decide if it is just a
horse or if it could possibly be a more magical
creature.

If you run after the animal, turn to page 41.

*If you turn away and follow the silver strands,
turn to page 102.*

An enormous flash of lightning illuminates the cave, revealing a wizened old woman draped in purple velvet. "A visitor!" she exclaims, and the next thing you know, daylight has replaced the darkness.

"Congratulations!" she cackles. "It's been two hundred and sixty-one years since anyone has been able to find me! I hope I didn't scare you—I was just practicing my storms. For the life of me I can't get the thunder to work!"

You open your mouth to say hello, but instead of your voice, a deep rumble of thunder emerges from the back of your throat.

"There's the thunder!" she shrieks gleefully.

You are afraid to open your mouth again. "Don't be shy," says the sorceress warmly. "I want to know why you've come."

Hesitantly you part your lips a bit. No thunder roars, so you tell the sorceress about the tainted water in your village well.

She shakes her head. "Sorry to disappoint you, but I can't clean up that mess in your well. Water is not my domain. Never has been, never will be. Why, I can't even create rain to go with my thunder and lightning!"

Turn to page 28.

The cave is so dark, you can't see where you're walking. You grope along slowly. Suddenly you feel a stone wobble beneath your feet. You find yourself plunging through the blackness deep into the earth.

Four hundred fifty years later a team of geologists discovers your skeleton. They spend several days trying to figure out what you were doing in such a deep chasm but are unable to reach a conclusion.

The End

After Simon rides away, you spend a few hours exploring the neighborhood. At dusk you return to the Duchess's house and curl up on the hard bench for the evening.

The next morning you awaken in a gloomy mood. You did not sleep well, and the rumbling of your stomach reminds you there is nothing for breakfast. Just then an approaching procession of overflowing carts and grand carriages drawn by well-groomed horses catches your attention. As the entourage stops in front of the house, the guards by the door stand even straighter.

You watch servants help an elegantly dressed woman step down from the most richly decorated of the carriages. Her jewel-studded bracelet glitters as she smoothes her velvet robe before entering the house. Servants unload cart after cart, carrying heavy wooden chests, bolts of brocade cloth, and—your heart skips a beat—a long, shimmering horn that is almost as tall as you are. It could only be a unicorn horn!

You wait until the two guards are distracted in conversation, then slip into the crowd of servants and carry one of the many chests into the house. You try not to appear too curious, but the splendid furnishings almost take your breath away. Passing one chamber, you glimpse the Duchess inside, sipping wine. The unicorn horn rests on the table before her. You put down the chest and enter the room.

Turn to page 43.

Riding through Arras, you enjoy watching the city people bustle about in their fancy but dust-covered clothing. Finally the cart stops at the tapestry workshop. Simon leads you into a large, bright room filled with looms, each holding a portion of a woven scene. "These tapestries will hang in the castles of kings!" he tells you. Although you know how to weave ordinary cloth, you have never seen a tapestry before.

The two of you walk over to one loom on which a few weavers are creating a huge tapestry showing a knight. "I'm looking for a weaver named Emil. Does any of you know him?" asks Simon.

One of the men smiles and points to his chest. "You've found him."

Turn to page 42.

The sound of water becomes more distinct as you creep steadily through the passageway. You are so intent on following the sound that you barely notice the spiders or the dusty webs anymore.

At last the light of your lantern flashes brightly on a rushing underground stream. The water smells fresh, so you taste it. You shriek with delight, for the water is sweet and very cold.

Your discovery of the stream saves your village. You and your friends manage to divert the flow so it runs directly under the trap door in the church. Although it makes a peculiar well, everyone is too happy to care.

The End

Emil gives you a small loom and a basket of white yarn. "Much of the magic of the tapestry comes from the dyes you will use to color the yarn before you begin to weave. I will give you instructions, but you must gather the special plants for the dyes yourself. You probably know most of the plants, but moon root is quite extraordinary." He hands you a drawing of the strange herb.

"Moon root? I've never heard of it. No one in my village uses it to dye clothing."

Emil laughs. "Moon root is so rare that not even the king's robes are dyed with it. You see, the plant only blossoms under a full moon. Luckily for you, tonight is the full moon."

That evening, you make your way through the forest outside the city to a certain grove of birch trees, where Emil suggested you look for moon root. You are delighted to see the peculiar, silvery plants growing there. Just as you begin to gather them a grotesque griffin descends noisily through the trees, heading straight for the precious moon root!

If you step forward to fight off the griffin, turn to page 101.

If you hide and watch to see what the griffin is up to, turn to page 67.

The white horse gallops so awkwardly that you have little trouble catching up with it. You grab its mane and throw your arms around its slender neck. Only then do you notice the small stump on the top of its head.

"You're hurting me," gasps the creature.

You are shocked by the animal's voice. "Are you some kind of magic horse—or a hornless unicorn?"

"I'm a unicorn, and if you'll release me, I'll tell you why my horn is missing."

You let go of the unicorn and smooth its tangled mane. "I'm sorry. I didn't mean to hurt you."

"Normally I could shake you right off. But several hours ago the warlock—the terror of this forest—cut off my horn. Without it I have no magic or strength. I'll be dead by daybreak."

"Oh, no!" you cry.

Part of you feels compelled to help the unicorn, or at least stay with it through the night. Yet another part of you wants to look for the warlock before he gets too far away with the horn.

If you decide to help the unicorn, turn to page 66.

If you ask the unicorn, "Where can I find the warlock?" turn to page 62.

Simon nudges you forward. "I want to find a unicorn," you explain. "The water in my village's well is tainted, and we might not last the summer unless it is purified. I'm told the touch of a unicorn's horn will clean it."

"You've come to the right man," says Emil. You say good-bye to Simon as Emil takes you aside. "I know two solutions to your problem, but neither is easy," Emil tells you. "I've heard one may obtain a unicorn by performing a ritual called the Circle of Wishes. However, it is very difficult and may cause you great anguish. The other way to clean your well is to weave a magic tapestry, and I can show you how to do that. It will take a full month to make. Once you complete it, you simply float the tapestry in the well, and the water will become pure."

The Circle of Wishes sounds frightening to you, but time is short. Can your village survive during the month required to weave the magic tapestry?

If you say, "Please tell me how to perform the Circle of Wishes," turn to page 46.

If you decide to weave the magic tapestry, turn to page 39.

Bowing deeply to the Duchess, you say, "Please excuse my boldness, but I've traveled a long way to ask this favor."

"Get out of here!" the Duchess snaps at you.

"Please hear me out," you say. "I just want to borrow your unicorn horn. My village needs your help!"

The Duchess looks at you coldly. "That is not my concern."

"I promise I'll return it," you insist.

She lowers her goblet to the table. "Please leave, or I shall call my guards to escort you."

As you trudge through the corridors you find yourself thinking about stealing the unicorn horn. Although you would do almost anything to save your village, you're not sure you could escape with something as large as the horn. And you hate to think what would happen if you were caught!

But then you notice a door inscribed with a golden sun. What could be behind such a magnificent door? you wonder. Since the door is slightly ajar, you peek inside. The room is filled with shelf after shelf of neatly labeled flasks and urns. Squinting your eyes, you see the vessels contain strange powders and wonder if any of the powders can purify water. Part of you wants to go inside to investigate, but another part of you thinks you should concentrate on getting the unicorn horn.

---

*If you open the door and go inside,
turn to page 92.*

*If you decide to steal the unicorn horn,
turn to page 97.*

"Even if you can't find a unicorn, you'll have fun talking with other animals," says the sorceress. She scoops a handful of brown flakes from a basket.

"What is that?"

"Ears and tongues from twelve creatures," she explains. You look away with disgust as she puts the flakes into a bowl and crushes them into a powder.

"Ready?" The sorceress carefully spoons the powder into each of your ears. "Open your mouth. Now, don't worry. This will dissolve, and you won't taste it at all." She places a dab under your tongue. "You can barely tell it's there."

"How do I know if it works?"

"Go ahead and try it!" she suggests. "Call my bat."

"Bat! Hey, bat!" you shout, feeling a little silly.

Within seconds the creature flutters toward you and squeaks, "You called?"

"Please lead me to the forest." You thank the sorceress, then follow the bat out of the cave and through the hills to the edge of the moonlit forest. There you say good-bye to the bat.

Hearing a rustling in the branches above, you call, "Hello?"

Go on to the next page.

An owl swoops out of the darkness, startling you as it lands on your shoulder. "Yooou must be a friend of the sorceress," it hoots.

"Yes, I am. The well in my village is tainted, so I'm looking for a unicorn to clean the water."

"Yooou'll have to decide whether you want just the horn or the unicorn itself," says the owl.

"Why?"

"This afternoon a warlock cut off the horn of the only unicorn I know. I'm not sure how magical the unicorn is without it, but I'm willing to bet the horn hasn't made the warlock any less wicked. That demon isn't going to be eager to lend you his new treasure. I can lead you to either, but neither one may be useful."

If you answer, "Please take me to the unicorn,"
turn to page 53.

If you are determined to get the magic horn
from the warlock, turn to page 54.

"The Circle of Wishes must take place at night," says Emil. "Since you'll need all the strength you possess, you should rest until the sun sets."

That evening Emil leads you away from the city, through the forest to a moonlit clearing. Countless small stones mark a wide circle. "Step inside," says Emil.

A shiver runs up your spine as you stand in the center. "Think of every wish in your heart and cast it out," instructs Emil.

"Cast it out?"

"Yes. Speak it aloud, and convince yourself you no longer desire that wish. You must continue until the last wish is gone from your heart."

"That's not so hard," you exclaim with relief. Emil does not reply. You think for a moment, then say, "I no longer wish for a horse of my own." As soon as the words leave your lips one of the stones of the circle glows and sparkles like a diamond. "I no longer wish to grow tall." A second stone begins to shimmer, and you realize that growing tall no longer matters to you.

As the hours pass you cast out hundreds of wishes, but the circle is still not fully illuminated. "Come on," urges Emil. "Do the hard ones."

Turn to page 52.

"I haven't made this kind of net for a few centuries," the sorceress warns. "I hope it works."

She sprinkles some herbs into a pot over the fire. "Blood of a griffin, scales of a dragon," she recites as she continues to add ingredients, "and a unicorn's eyelash." She stirs the concoction and tosses in some gold powder.

The sorceress dips a pair of knitting needles in the simmering potion. Your eyes widen with amazement as you watch her swiftly knit a sparkling net.

"There." She sighs. "Now use it carefully. This net can snare any magical creature, not just a unicorn."

The sorceress leads you out of her cave. When she sees night has fallen, she says, "Are you sure you want to begin your search now? You can come back to the cave with me and get a fresh start in the morning."

"Thank you for everything," you reply, "but I think there's enough moonlight for me to see where I'm going." You wave good-bye and set off for the forest.

You are walking through a thicket of pines when you realize you forgot to ask the sorceress how to use the net. Should you set a trap with it or try to cast it over the unicorn once you find it?

If you decide this is a perfect spot to construct a trap with the net, turn to page 61.

If you think it's better to wait until you see a unicorn to use the net, turn to page 58.

50

"Could you tell me where that bat went?" you ask Brother Michel as you climb down.

He dashes out and hurries back. "It's sitting on the ledge outside that window!"

You swing the rope toward the rafter and jump onto the beam. The bell clangs crazily.

"I'll distract the villagers so they don't scare the bat away," Brother Michel tells you.

You thank him. "I'm going to lower myself onto the windowsill, then go out on the ledge," you say.

Taking a deep breath, you step through the window onto the narrow wooden ledge. The sun-scorched wood feels hot on your bare feet. You flatten your back against the building and try to control the dizziness that threatens to overwhelm you. The bat cocks its head at you expectantly, then flutters further along the ledge. You are terrified to take another step. You squeeze your eyes shut, conscious only of the blood pounding in your ears.

Turn to page 56.

As you search through the forest for silver strands you hear a rustling of leaves. Stepping quietly, you follow the sound until you spy a flash of silver through the trees.

It is not a unicorn after all, but a young woman wearing a fraying shawl woven of silver thread. As you run up to her you wonder if she might be the sorceress, for no ordinary person would own such a shawl.

"Hello!" you call.

When she turns around, you see her face is filled with terror. Her velvet gown is torn and dusty. "I thought you were the kidnappers," she explains breathlessly.

"What kidnappers?" you ask.

"Those villains who kidnapped me. I managed to escape during the night, but I'm sure they're looking for me." She glances around nervously. "Can you hide me?"

"Sure," you reply, "I'll bring you home to my village."

She smiles at you gratefully. "I'm so lucky you found me! What are you doing in the middle of the forest anyway? You don't look like a hunter or a woodcutter."

Turn to page 57.

You take a deep breath. "I don't care if our crops fail. I no longer wish for a healthy life. I no longer wish my parents were alive." You name more and more wishes until only two stones remain. You are so exhausted, you have trouble thinking of any other wishes.

"Okay," you say, sighing. "I no longer wish to save my village from the drought."

"Good," says Emil, "just one more."

"That was it," you insist. "I have no more desires."

"Yes, there is one more."

"No."

"Your life," he reminds you. "Cast away your desire to live."

Although you feel curiously empty, your wish to continue living is strong. You are not sure you can pluck it from your heart.

If you refuse to abandon this last desire, turn to page 73.

If you resolve to cast out your will to live, turn to page 65.

The owl flaps its wings. "Tooo the unicorn!"

You hurry after the owl, stumbling on roots and thrashing through brambles. "Slow down!" you call. "I can't see in the dark as well as you can!"

"Huuuman beings!" hoots the owl scornfully. "Why don't you sleep now, and we'll go to the unicorn in the morning?"

"Good idea," you reply. You curl up at the foot of an oak tree and soon drift into a deep and dreamless sleep.

When you awake the next morning, the owl is perched on your shoulder. "I'm so glad you suggested I rest," you say as you stretch your arms. "I feel great!"

"Gooood. Now, let's get going. You can eat some berries along the way."

Turn to page 24.

"It's the magic horn I need, not the rest of the unicorn," you tell the owl. "I want to meet the warlock."

"Follooow me!" The owl leads you along a dry streambed, where water flowed before the drought. After walking a few miles, you spot the flickering of a campfire. Squinting your eyes, you can just make out a small figure dancing around the flames.

"Is that the warlock?"

"Loooower your voice!" scolds the owl. "He has extraordinary hearing and the sharpest of eyes!"

When you are finally close enough to get a good look, a tight knot of panic forms in your stomach. The warlock's eyes glow red in the darkness, and his gleeful howls strike terror in your heart.

"Well, I guess I'll just have to ask if he'll lend me the unicorn horn," you whisper to the owl.

"Hooow many times do I have to tell you? He isn't a kindhearted soul. In fact, he has no heart at all."

"He's not much taller than me. Maybe I can sneak up on him and wrestle him to the ground," you suggest. "Then I can grab the horn and run away before he can stand up." You sound more confident than you really feel.

"Are you suuure? The warlock won't hesitate to use magic to win a battle," warns the owl.

If you decide to reason with the warlock, turn to page 68.

If you think you are strong enough to overpower the warlock, turn to page 80.

You finally force yourself to open your eyes. The bat is still waiting. As you edge toward it an enormous splinter pierces your foot. Unbearable pain pulses up your leg, filling your entire body. Your leg jerks into the air and your arms fly out in a desperate attempt to steady yourself, but there is nothing to grab. You scream with horror as you plummet to the ground.

When you regain consciousness, a crowd of villagers is gathered around you. "You're alive, thank heaven," cries Marie-Claire.

"Yes, but you've broken both your legs," says Brother Michel.

You know your search for the sorceress is over.

The End

You sigh wearily. "I'm looking for a unicorn. You see, the well in my village is tainted, and our supply of rainwater is almost gone."

"I can help you," says the woman happily.

"You can?"

She looks at you strangely. "Don't you know who I am?"

You shake your head.

"I'm the king's daughter," she replies, "and just as soon as I get home, I'll give you my unicorn horn as a reward for saving me."

The End

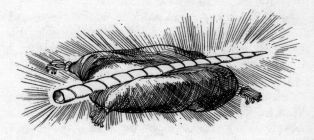

You walk through the moonlit forest, searching for the unicorn. Finally you become too tired to continue. You curl up beneath a pine tree and fall asleep, clutching the golden net tightly.

As you float in and out of dreams you sense someone—or something—watching you. Opening one eye, you see a small white horse sniffing the net. You sit up, and the horse skitters back with fear.

"It's okay," you whisper, holding out your hand. "Come here, horse."

The animal draws its head up proudly and says softly, "Maybe you can't recognize me without my horn, but I'm still a unicorn."

"I didn't know unicorns could talk!" you exclaim.

"We do many things people don't know about," the unicorn answers.

"What happened to your horn?"

"Just this morning, a warlock attacked me and cut it off," the unicorn explains sadly. "You see, the horn holds my magic. Without it I'll die by dawn."

"That's terrible!" you cry. "Could a sorceress save you?"

"Maybe," answers the unicorn. "I know one ritual to restore my horn, but I can't perform it myself. A sorceress might be able to help, but there's so little time."

"Tell me about this ritual," you urge the unicorn.

Go on to the next page.

"It's called the Rainbow of Tears. It takes thousands of teardrops under the light of the moon to form the rainbow," says the unicorn.

You want to help the unicorn but aren't sure whether you should run back for the sorceress or try to think of a way of creating the Rainbow of Tears yourself.

*If you decide to ask the sorceress for help,
turn to page 74.*

*If you offer to create the Rainbow of Tears,
turn to page 79.*

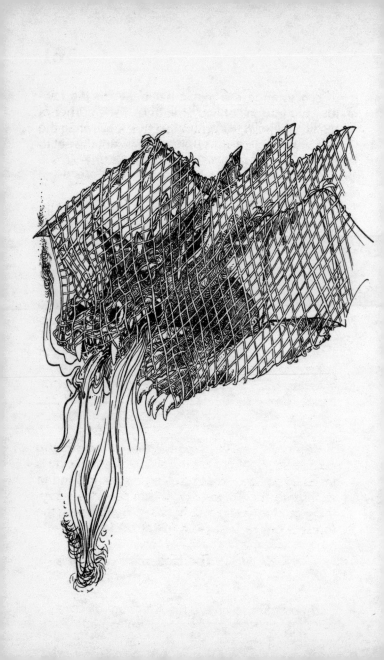

You arrange the magic net between the low-hanging boughs of two pine trees. One corner of the net trails on the ground so that it will snag the hoof of the unicorn and cause the rest of the net to descend upon the unsuspecting creature. It is a pretty clever trap, you decide, but it needs some delicious bait to attract a unicorn.

As you rove through the moonlit forest you try to imagine what unicorns like to eat. The heady fragrance of honeysuckle makes you think the sweet nectar inside the blossoms might be tempting bait. You pick an armful of the yellow flowers and spread them under the net. Feeling very satisfied, you hide in a nearby grove of ferns to watch and wait. Time passes slowly in the darkness. Despite your intentions, you fall sound asleep.

A few hours later fierce screeches interrupt your dreams. You run to the trap. Much to your horror you discover not a unicorn, but a raging dragon snarled in the magic net! You have to get it off the monster or you won't be able to use it to catch a unicorn.

When you walk toward the net, the dragon emits a scorching blast of fire. Your entire body is instantly ablaze. You try rolling on the ground to extinguish the flames, but within seconds everything around you is also burning. By morning the forest is only a vast plain full of cinders.

The End

"The warlock is hard to find because he's always moving around," answers the unicorn. "The sparrows have told me he often visits the wood-witch who lives west of here, where the fir trees grow."

"How will I recognize her?" you ask.

The unicorn shrugs weakly. "I've never seen her myself. There's enough danger in this forest already. I don't go looking for more."

As you thank the unicorn you feel a twinge of guilt for abandoning it. But you remind yourself that saving your village is the most important thing right now.

All through the night you head west. By dawn you notice more and more fir trees growing among the birches and maples. A soft wailing sends a chill up your spine. You tell yourself it must be the wind.

Turn to page 70.

"I'll miss you, too," you tell Emil, "but I have to go home. I'll always be grateful for your help."

Emil gives you money to pay someone to drive you and the magic tapestry home. You ask the driver to let you off just outside your village, where you patiently wait until everyone is asleep. You hope your neighbors will put aside their fears of leprosy when they discover you've purified the water.

Quietly you drag the heavy tapestry to the well. When you unroll it, you see it now shows a unicorn dipping its horn into your well. You shove the tapestry in and listen for a splash as it hits the water. Then you lower a bucket and pull up some water. It smells fresh and tastes better than ever.

At dawn you run to Marie-Claire's house and wake her up. She hugs you joyfully as you cry, "Come outside! Taste the water! I've made it pure!"

She drinks the fresh water and you tell her about the magic tapestry. "But where is it?" asks Marie-Claire, peering into the well.

You gaze into the water. All you see is the reflection of the moon in the early-morning sky.

The End

Summoning all your strength, you whisper, "I cast away my wish to live."

The last stone brightens.

"Now step outside the circle," says Emil.

As you cross the glowing boundary you are transformed into a unicorn. You gaze at your silvery hoofs in astonishment, then toss your head to feel the weight of your long horn. Without wasting any time, you set out for your village.

The next day, when you arrive home at twilight, most of the villagers are in their houses. You trot over to Marie-Claire's cottage and poke your head through her doorway.

She looks up from her sewing and gasps, "What in the world . . ."

"It's me! I'm back," you say.

Marie-Claire touches the good-luck pendant still hanging from your neck. "It *is* you! What happened? You were going to find a unicorn, not turn into one!"

"I'll tell you all about it later. First let's go out to the well and see if this horn of mine really does work!"

The End

"What can I do to help?" you ask the unicorn.

The unicorn sighs. "There is only one way you can save me, and even then I'm not sure it will work."

"Tell me what it is!"

"When thousands of teardrops are combined with moonlight," explains the unicorn, "they form a Rainbow of Tears, which has special healing power for unicorns."

"I'll do it!" you exclaim eagerly.

"It's kind of you to offer, but the rainbow probably requires more tears than you can weep."

"You'd be surprised how much I can cry!" you insist.

"It takes thousands of tears," the unicorn reminds you.

"I could run home to get my friends to help too," you suggest, although you're not really sure anyone in the village will listen to you.

The unicorn shakes its head sadly. "There is so little time. Remember, by dawn I'll be dead."

If you decide to cry the Rainbow of Tears yourself, turn to page 99.

If you decide to bring your friends to help cry for the unicorn, turn to page 110.

You jump quickly into some dense raspberry bushes where you can safely watch the griffin. The beast sniffs the plants and begins gobbling them with alarming speed.

You have to stop the griffin from devouring all the moon root, or you'll have to wait another month for it to blossom again. As you struggle to decide what to do you nervously pop raspberries in your mouth. Their sweet taste gives you an idea.

You fill your hands with the ripest berries. Quietly placing them on the ground, you form a trail from the bushes to the birch grove. The griffin is so busy consuming the moon root that it doesn't notice your approach.

Taking careful aim, you toss a raspberry towards the griffin. The beast eats it eagerly and looks around for another. You toss a second berry, and the griffin snatches it up. You continue to throw berries, making sure each one lands a bit closer than the last to your trail. Just as the griffin discovers the trail of raspberries you duck behind a shrub. Distracted by the berries, the beast moves away from the moon root. You breathlessly gather the remaining plants.

Turn to page 85.

"I'll ask the warlock to lend me the unicorn horn," you announce. Although you try to sound casual, your hands are trembling.

"Gooood luck!" says the owl. "I'll wait here."

You walk closer to the campfire before calling, "Hello!"

The warlock abruptly stops dancing. As he strides toward you his glowing red eyes are fixed on Marie-Claire's talisman. You slowly extend both hands, palms up, to show you have no weapons. The warlock studies you warily, then shakes your hand. You try not to shudder as his hot, blistered hand touches yours.

After describing the danger facing your village, you ask if he would lend you his unicorn horn.

The warlock laughs sourly. "Between the world of angels and the land of demons, there is no one who will ever touch my unicorn horn. Banish that idea from your mind immediately!"

"But . . ."

A sly grin spreads across the warlock's face. "For a certain price I could concoct a potion to clean your well."

"I have no money."

"It's not money I want." The warlock stares intently at the pendant hanging from your neck. "Where did you get that?"

"From my friend Marie-Claire."

"Give it to me, and I'll mix the potion for you."

Turn to page 78.

"I'm going to see what's behind the trap door," you tell Brother Michel.

"I'll keep the villagers outside so they won't distract you," he calls to you. "Be careful!"

The bell rings loudly as you climb up the rope. At the top you crawl through the opening into a small, dark compartment. The tiny room is empty save for a large goblet brimming with a clear, colorless liquid. Hesitantly you take a sip. When you realize it is fresh, cool water, you take several sizable gulps. You pause for a second and notice the goblet is just as full as it was when you first discovered it.

Being careful not to drop the glass, you climb down from the steeple. Quite a bit of water spills on the way, but the goblet remains full. You rush outside to show Brother Michel, and find the entire village gathered with him.

"Look what I discovered!" you shout. You pass the goblet among the puzzled villagers. They each take a drink and marvel at the endless supply of water.

Brother Michel shakes his head with disbelief. "My grandmother's great-grandmother told her a saint had blessed our village with a secret treasure," he tells you. "All my life I've tried to figure out what it was. You've found it!"

Before you know what is happening, you find yourself on the shoulders of your friends and neighbors. The crowd cheers your cleverness and courage as they march toward their parched fields with the magic goblet.

The End

Farther ahead, past a stand of fir trees, you see a clearing. You race up to it, expecting to find the wood-witch's dwelling. Instead, you discover seven life-size wooden statues! Most are of surprised woodcutters, but there is also a crying child and another statue of a woman. Her face is full of terror. You study them closely, noticing that some are remarkably detailed, while others seem more like fir trees than humans.

The sudden crack of a breaking twig makes you turn sharply. A tall creature, half-woman, half-trees, stares at you with glittering green eyes. Two branches move like arms to embrace you. "Run," you tell yourself, but you can't. You are paralyzed with fear.

"Don't be frightened," whispers the wood-witch. As she touches you, your body turns to wood. You can't see a thing, but you can think and feel, and your screams sound like the howl of the wind.

"You make a lovely statue," says the witch as she strokes your smooth wooden arm. "And in ten or twenty years you'll be a handsome fir tree."

The End

"No, I can't make the trade," you tell the merchant. "The survival of my village depends on the unicorn horn."

The merchant sighs. "I understand your reluctance, but believe me, you're making a mistake. Now tell me about that pendant you're wearing."

"It belongs to an old woman in my village," you answer. "It's her good-luck charm."

"I'll tell you what—if you give me the pendant, I'll trade you my horse."

"Why would you give me a horse for a glass charm?" you ask warily.

"If I'm not mistaken, that talisman has untapped magical possibilities. I'd like to have it for my collection," says the merchant. "My horse, on the other hand, is disappointingly ordinary. Of course, I was led to believe it was an enchanted beast, but that's a whole other story."

Turn to page 83.

"I won't do it. I can't give up my will to live," you say.

As you begin to step outside the glowing circle, Emil shouts, "Stop! You can't leave the circle now!"

It is too late. When your foot touches the ground, you abruptly disappear in a flash of lightning. Emil claps his hands over his ears to muffle the deafening roar of thunder. Rain rushes from the night sky, drenching the forest, the city, and all of Flanders, including your parched village.

People everywhere rush outside with buckets and bowls. They turn their faces up to the long-awaited rain. You never feel a single drop, however, for you have vanished forever.

The End

You race through the forest to get the sorceress. When you finally reach her chamber in the hills, the only thing you can see is a swarm of lavender moths glowing in the darkness.

"Help! Help! The unicorn needs you!" you shout at the moths. You feel silly talking to a bunch of insects and hope it's another of the sorceress's forms.

The moths abruptly disappear. "Great galloping goblins!" exclaims the sorceress. "Just hold on while I find the light."

The rich colors of a sunset suddenly fill the cave. "Wrong one!" she snaps. The next thing you know, it is broad daylight, and the sorceress stands before you in her purple robe. You explain breathlessly what has happened to the unicorn.

"That's terrible!" she replies. "Fortunately I know two spells that *may* work. I could transform the unicorn back to a baby—when it still had its horn—or I could apply a healing potion to make the horn grow back. I must warn you, both potions are very tricky. Every now and then the baby concoction turns into an old-age spell instead."

"And what about the healing potion?" you ask.

Go on to the next page.

"Well, sometimes things grow back differently. The horn could grow back as a butterfly's antenna or a deer's antler. The real problem is that neither of these spells is reversible, and I certainly don't want to be responsible for what happens. The choice is up to you."

If you answer, "Please make the unicorn a baby again," turn to page 81.

If you tell the sorceress to try the healing potion, turn to page 93.

As you make your way through the narrow tunnel formed by the bat, you notice the passageway slopes deeper into the earth. The space becomes so small that you have to slide slowly along on your stomach. After wriggling for what seems like half a mile, you know you must be far away from the church.

Suddenly thick shrouds of cobwebs block the tunnel ahead. There isn't a trace of the bat. You cover your eyes with one arm and push through the webs with another. When you lower your arm from your face, you find you are inches away from the most enormous spider you have ever seen. It is even bigger than a rat.

The giant spider springs on you! Forgetting the low ceiling, forgetting everything except the eight hairy legs clutching your shoulders and face, you bolt upright. Your head smashes against the earth above. Before you know what is happening, the ceiling collapses. Still locked in the spider's deadly grip, you are buried forever under tons of earth.

That night Brother Michel summons the courage to look for you, but his search yields no clue to your disappearance.

The End

You hesitate, but Marie-Claire's words—*"Use it as you need it"*—echo in your mind. You unclasp the charm and give it to the warlock.

He returns to his campsite and begins mixing the potion in a goatskin flask. He finally hands it to you and says, "Pour this in your well tomorrow night before the moon rises. By the time the moon sets, your water will be pure."

"Thank you!" You hurry back to the owl and gleefully shout, "Let's go! I'm going to save my village!"

And you do.

The End

You nervously twist the golden net while thinking of a solution. Looking down at the net, you exclaim, "I've got an idea!"

Without another word you race through the forest with the net unfurling like a sail behind you. Stomping your feet and thrashing past branches, you startle the birds out of their slumber. As they fearfully flutter into the air, their wings tangle in the magic net. With each bird it traps the net grows larger, until it holds thousands.

Exhausted but triumphant, you return to the unicorn, leading an enormous golden cloud of screeching birds. "Cry!" you shout. "Cry for the unicorn and cry for yourselves!"

Turn to page 113.

"I'm going to fight him," you tell the owl. "It's the only way I'll ever get the unicorn horn."

You creep closer to the whirling warlock, then duck behind a tree. Peering cautiously around the trunk, you spot the unicorn horn beside the warlock's dancing feet.

With more strength than you knew you possessed, you hurl yourself on the warlock's back. He stumbles, nearly falling to the ground, but quickly regains his balance and flips you over his head. You crash to the ground. The warlock roughly yanks you up again. Gripping your arms tightly, he stares into your eyes. The next thing you know, you are dancing feverishly, mesmerized by the fire in his red eyes.

The warlock blinks slowly a few times, and you find yourself growing very sleepy. You can barely keep your eyes open, let alone continue dancing. Overwhelmed by slumber, you are conscious only of the warlock's whisper in your ear.

"Sleep well, foolish urchin. You'll have five hundred years to dream."

The End

"I love this baby spell," says the sorceress gleefully. "I used it a lot when I was growing up. If my brothers or sisters annoyed me, I would just change them into infants. Why, one brother celebrated his first birthday twelve times!"

You laugh politely, but you're in a hurry to return to the unicorn.

The sorceress rummages through her supply baskets. "I'll need skin of the black snake, crumbled eggshells, and one more thing. What was it? Oh, yes, those dried flowers—baby's breath. All right, I'm ready."

"Should we bring a lantern?" you ask.

"There's no need," she replies. "I'll turn us both into the wind." She takes your hand, and before you know what is happening, you are nothing but air rushing through the darkness.

"To the left, past those rocks," you direct the sorceress. Within minutes you are there, back in human forms again.

The unicorn smiles with relief. "I didn't think you'd get here in time."

"Your worries are over," says the sorceress. She explains the spell and mixes the magical concoction. "This is ready for you to eat," she tells the unicorn.

Turn to page 86.

You hate to give away Marie-Claire's good-luck charm, but you realize you can't walk all the way home lugging the heavy unicorn horn.

"It's a deal," you announce, removing the pendant. You hand it to the merchant, who pockets it and removes his wares from his horse. Awkwardly clutching the unicorn horn, you climb into the horse's saddle.

Before you can even say good-bye, you find yourself riding off the ground, above the rooftops, and into the sky!

"Winking wizards!" shrieks the merchant. "That horse *is* magical!"

"Whoa!" you cry, tugging on the reins. The horse ignores you. With fear and fascination, you watch the world grow smaller and smaller. As the horse soars higher toward the stars you have to gasp for air. Just as you begin to faint, the unicorn horn tumbles from your hand. A second later you, too, are plunging toward the earth with deathly speed.

The End

"Thanks again," you tell the servant as he locks the iron door. Then you curl up in the straw for a nap.

When you awake, narrow stripes of moonlight fill the dungeon. You remember the piece of unicorn horn in your pocket and take it out for a closer look. It is too dark to see well, so you place the chunk of horn on the ledge of the window. You marvel at its pearly luster, trying to forget your hopeless situation.

The muffled sound of approaching hoofbeats distracts you. Through the window you glimpse silvery hoofs much too delicate to belong to a horse. You hold your breath, wondering if it could be a unicorn, as a shimmering horn dips between the bars of the window. For a moment the horn rests on the piece of unicorn horn on the ledge, then touches each of the bars, instantly transforming them into fragile rods of glass.

Turn to page 94.

The next morning Emil shows you how to combine the moon root with other plants to create magical dyes. You soak the yarn in the dye, stirring occasionally, just as you would at home. At first the resulting colors seem disappointingly ordinary, but when you examine them more closely, you discover the flash of rubies in the red yarn and the scent of pine in the green yarn. When you hold the blue yarn beside your ear, you hear the sound of rushing water.

Since you already know how to weave plain cloth, you have no trouble understanding Emil's instructions for making the tapestry. When you finally start to weave, it is even easier than you expected. The yarn seems to lead your fingers, creating a design of its own. While Emil weaves only an inch of a regular tapestry each day, you weave almost a foot of your magic tapestry.

Turn to page 90.

You watch expectantly as the unicorn laps up the potion. Almost immediately its horn grows back while its body shrinks.

"I feel wonderful!" exclaims the unicorn in a high, lilting voice. "I know my horn is powerful enough to clean your well, but I must admit, I'm afraid. Until my legs grow longer, I'll be easy prey for that warlock."

"I'll take care of you!" you offer eagerly. "You can live with me and be my pet."

The unicorn nuzzles you gratefully. "I was hoping you'd say that."

After the unicorn cleans the water in your well, the villagers adopt it as a mascot. It stays by your side for the rest of your life.

The End

Unknown to the Duchess, you become Marcel's apprentice while he tries to invent a metal to clean your well. You learn to create horseshoes that silence hoofbeats and scissors that sing. Marcel says you show great promise as an alchemist.

By October Marcel still hasn't invented a metal to purify water. Each night you tell yourself you'll go home the next day, but the next day always brings such intriguing problems and discoveries that you can't bear to leave. Besides, you dread finding what has become of your village.

You end up spending the rest of your life as an alchemist. Like Marcel, you invent dozens of astonishing metals. But you never find a way to purify water, and you never succeed in creating gold.

The End

One day toward the end of winter the peddler Simon stops by the studio with good news. "That tapestry of yours saved the village, all right!" he tells you. "Everyone is fine, although they miss you."

"So they still think about me?" you say, secretly pleased.

"They think about you every day," Simon assures you. "In fact, they're so grateful to you for saving them that they've changed the name of the village. They've named it after you!"

The End

As the days pass, you see the tapestry shows a unicorn dancing in the forest by the light of the moon. Each morning, when you resume weaving, you discover the moon is in a slightly different phase, and the unicorn is in another position. Emil assures you that the scenes in magic tapestries are always changing.

Finally, when you have finished weaving, you cut the tapestry off the loom and roll it up. You are eager to see if the tapestry really does purify water, but you are also sad to be leaving Emil. You've grown to like him and the other weavers.

When you say good-bye to Emil, he replies, "I wish you weren't leaving. You've learned so much, and I enjoy having you around. Why don't you send the tapestry home with a messenger and stay on here as a weaver?"

If you accept Emil's offer, turn to page 10.

If you decide to go back to the village, turn to page 63.

Inside the room, you find an old man heating a piece of wire over a candle. When he sees you, he nods pleasantly. You introduce yourself, and he tells you his name is Marcel.

"What are you doing?" you ask.

Marcel sighs. "Like all alchemists, I'm supposed to be finding a way to create gold. The trouble is, I seem to be creating everything *but* gold!" He shows you a silvery spoon. "This makes ordinary soup taste like nectar! And look at this ring. If you wear it on your finger, it will keep your whole hand warm. Why, I've invented hundreds of new metals, but the Duchess wants only gold."

"Have you ever created a metal that can purify water?" You explain the problem facing your village.

"Can't say I have," Marcel replies, "but it shouldn't be hard to make a water-cleaning metal. Let's work on that idea right away!"

Turn to page 88.

"Please mix the healing potion," you tell the sorceress. "And be careful! We don't want the horn to grow back as an antler."

"Don't worry." She measures the ingredients with maddening slowness and spends almost an hour stirring the potion. Every few minutes you dash outside the cave to see if it is dawn yet.

When the sorceress is finally finished, she says, "I'm going to turn us into swallows so we'll be able to reach the unicorn quickly."

"Into swallows?" All your life you've dreamed of flying!

"Sure. I'll put the vial of potion in a basket and carry it in my beak."

The sorceress brushes your neck with a swallow feather and murmurs a strange chant. You find you've become a bird, and you hop around the cave joyfully while the sorceress transforms herself.

You follow the sorceress out of the cave and then lead her toward the unicorn. As you soar exuberantly through the dark you realize flying is even more thrilling than you had imagined!

Turn to page 114.

Without thinking, you reach up and effortlessly break the glass bars. Only then do you wonder how you can hoist your body up to escape. As if in answer to your question the long white horn reappears through the window. It seems to beckon, so you grab hold of it and find yourself being pulled up and out of the dungeon.

You stumble to your feet and embrace the unicorn that saved you. You are surprised to hear the gentle creature murmur, "Climb on my back. I'll carry you home." You reach back through the window for the chunk of horn, then swing your leg over the slim back of the unicorn. The unicorn glides through the night toward your village.

The End

You curse your bad luck as you run past the men to the village. Marie-Claire's talisman has led to one misfortune after another, and this is the worst! When you reach the well, you tear the charm off your neck and hurl it into the murky water.

"Good riddance!" you yell. "You've brought me nothing but bad luck!"

You rub your eyes in disbelief. The water begins sparkling brightly. You can see clear to the bottom of the well!

"It's clean!" you shout jubilantly. "The water is clean!"

The villagers gather around the well to taste the fresh water. "Welcome home!" they cheer.

The End

You walk back to the chamber where you last saw the Duchess and duck behind one of the huge tapestries hanging in the hallway outside. You wait patiently until you hear the Duchess leave the room. When you peer into the chamber, you are relieved to see the unicorn horn still lying on the table. Without a moment's hesitation you grab the heavy horn and run—smack into the Duchess herself!

"Guards!" she screams.

The next thing you know, a dozen guards are angrily pursuing you through the winding corridors of the Duchess's house. To your horror you realize you can't remember the way out. Can you continue running with the horn until you reach a door, or should you try to hide from the guards?

If you keep running, turn to page 105.

If you hide, turn to page 103.

"It's a deal." You offer the merchant the unicorn horn as he places the magic opals in your hand. The stones make your palm tingle.

"How do these work?" you ask.

"Hold one opal at a time against your forehead and speak your wish," answers the merchant.

You put two of the opals in your pocket and hold the third against your forehead. Closing your eyes, you whisper, "Please make the water in my village's well perfectly pure." You find yourself envisioning the rank and murky water clearing. You see yourself sipping the fresh water. You feel confident your wish has been granted.

When you open your eyes, you notice the merchant has mounted his horse. "Good luck!" he calls as he rides away with the unicorn horn.

Taking a second opal, you wish your parents were alive. In your mind's eye you see a young couple entering your village. You know right away they are your parents, even though you have no memory of their faces. You can't wait to get home!

With growing excitement you reach for the third opal. Pressing it against your forehead, you murmur, "Please make the villagers willing to let me come home." You breathe a sigh of relief, for suddenly you feel certain your neighbors will welcome you back.

You carefully pocket the opals and begin the long journey home.

The End

"Let me try to cry the Rainbow of Tears," you insist.

"I'm touched by your kindness and courage." The unicorn glances at the sky. "The moon will rise in a few hours. Until then just rest."

When darkness cloaks the forest and the moon is high, the unicorn murmurs, "It is time."

You remind yourself of every unhappiness you've ever experienced and tears begin to trickle down your cheeks. Then you imagine all kinds of misfortunes that could happen in the future. You sob uncontrollably as tears drip off your nose and chin, soaking your shirt. You cry so hard, you begin to cough, but nothing happens. No matter how much you weep, no rainbow appears.

"I'm sorry it isn't working," you whisper to the unicorn.

"No one can fault you for trying." The unicorn rests its head on your lap. As morning approaches it begins to croon sorrowfully. The unicorn's song of death pierces through the darkness, penetrating the dreams of people far and wide.

With the first blush of dawn the unicorn's voice falters, and you notice the sound of galloping hoofs. Before you have a chance to wonder who is approaching, a unicorn plunges through the shrubs. It halts beside you and lowers its lustrous horn to touch the head of the dying unicorn. Their eyes meet. You watch the unicorn in your lap smile peacefully, then close its eyes for the last time.

Turn to page 104.

You wave your arms frantically to scare off the griffin. Not at all bothered by your efforts, the beast sinks its claws into one of your arms. You try to ignore the pain, and with your uninjured arm you struggle bravely to free yourself from the creature's grip. With the last of your strength you try to fling off the griffin. You lose your balance and topple into the moon root. The griffin's gleaming claws are inches from your face when you close your eyes.

The End

Although you try to retrace your steps carefully, you can't find any more strands of silver. After several hours of searching, you stop at a small pond for a drink of water. But when you look more closely, you are repelled by a thick layer of scum floating on the surface. Tired and thirsty, you sit down beside the pond to rest.

As you try to decide what to do next you pluck a pod from a peculiar plant that you've never seen before. You open the pod and idly toss the seeds one by one onto the stagnant pond. You blink with disbelief as the water suddenly begins to sparkle!

Quickly tearing open another pod, you throw a seed into the pond. You watch with amazement as the water becomes so clear, you can see the bottom. When you take a sip, you find it is as fresh as you could ever want. Breathless with excitement, you gather as many of the strange pods as you can find.

The villagers accept you back when they learn you can purify the water. By keeping the location of the plants a secret, you eventually earn a small fortune purifying other wells with the mysterious seeds. Before long your seeds replace unicorn horns as the most highly regarded method of purifying water.

The End

Still clutching the unicorn horn, you climb quickly into a big wooden trunk and lower the lid. Your heart is pounding so loudly, you fear the guards will hear it, but the thunder of their footsteps doesn't slow as they race by you. When all is quiet, you try to find a comfortable position within your cramped hiding place.

You can't tell how much time passes. To your hungry stomach it feels like centuries. You slowly open the lid a bit and peer out. The hallway is dark.

You climb out and carry the unicorn horn into the nearest room. Very quietly you open the shutters of a window and look outside. To your relief it is not far to the ground, and there is no one in sight. You hold the horn tightly and leap from the window. A broad hedge cushions your landing.

You hurry through the dark and silent streets of Arras, guided by the soft glow of the heavy unicorn horn. At the sound of approaching hoofbeats you duck into a doorway. You try to shield the light of the horn with your body, but it is impossible to conceal. The rider spots you immediately. He comes closer for a better look, cornering you in the doorway.

Turn to page 108.

The second unicorn raises its head and says, "Thank you for staying with my sister. Is there anything I can do to repay you?"

"As a matter of fact, there is." You describe the problem facing your village.

"Climb on my back and show me the way," replies the unicorn.

You clutch its mane as the unicorn races through the forest toward your village.

The End

Determined to find a way out, you race even faster. You don't notice how slippery the rugs are until it is too late.

As you stumble the unicorn horn falls from your hand, crashing onto the hard marble floor. It shatters into hundreds of pieces. You sink to your knees in despair. Just as you hear the guards approaching, you quickly snatch a piece of the broken horn and hide it in your pocket.

The next thing you know, the guards are hustling you down the stairs to a small underground dungeon. The iron door clangs shut, and you hear a key clicking in the lock. The dungeon is empty save for a pile of dusty straw. Just above your head a barred window offers a view of the ground outside the house.

Go on to the next page.

After several hours a hunchbacked old servant unlocks the door and offers you a hunk of bread. You eagerly accept it and thank him.

"I'll bring you more in the morning," he tells you. "It's not much, but I can't sneak anything else past the cook."

"You mean, you're not supposed to be feeding me?"

"Of course not!" he exclaims. "The Duchess doesn't waste food on prisoners, but I can't stand the thought of someone starving to death right under my nose."

As you chew the bread a plan takes shape in your mind. If you offer to share the piece of unicorn horn in your pocket with the old man, will he let you escape? You are desperate to leave the dungeon but are not sure how much you can trust him.

If you try to bribe the man, turn to page 111.

If you think it's too soon to take any chances, turn to page 84.

108

"I won't ask how you acquired it, but tell me, is that a unicorn horn you're hiding?" The rider leans down from his horse, straining to see.

"Who are you?" you ask, noticing the silver stars embroidered on his coat.

"I'm a merchant of magic, a purveyor of possibility, and I'd give anything to have a unicorn horn among my wares. In fact, I can make you a most attractive offer."

"I'm not interested." Behind your back, you grip the horn more tightly.

"Just listen. I have three splendid opals, each of which can grant you one wish. Imagine—three of your dearest dreams can be transformed into reality!" He pauses to dismount, knowing he has aroused your interest. "The catch is, you can use the opals only once; then you must share them with another person. I've already had my wishes. I'll trade you not one, not two, but all three opals for that unicorn horn you're clutching." He reaches into a blue velvet pouch and displays three gleaming opals. They are the color of moonlight but glow with the brilliance of the sun. You can't take your eyes away from them.

"How do I know these are really magic?"

Go on to the next page.

The merchant sighs. "Trust me. Do these look like ordinary opals to you?"

You've never seen ordinary opals before, so you can't tell. The possibility of having three wishes come true is almost irresistible, yet you can't be certain the merchant is telling the truth.

If you decide to accept his word, turn to page 98.

If you think it's too risky a trade, turn to page 72.

"I'll hurry back," you promise the unicorn as you set out for your village. The shadows grow longer with each step you take. You search anxiously for familiar sights, but by the time the moon rises, you know you are lost. You decide to return to the unicorn, but after walking all night, you find no trace of it.

By morning you know that the unicorn must be dead. Holding Marie-Claire's talisman in your hands, you whisper to it, "If you really bring good luck, prove it to me now. Help me find my way home."

For three long days you stumble aimlessly through the forest. Just as you begin to think you are lost forever, you hear voices in the distance. You discover two of your neighbors working in their field! You are so relieved, you forget about their fears of leprosy and rush over to greet them.

"Get away!" shouts one.

"You can't come back!" cries the other.

Turn to page 95.

You remove the piece of unicorn horn from your pocket and show it to the servant.

"If you let me out of this dungeon, I will give you half of this piece of unicorn horn."

The servant's eyes widen. "How did you get that?"

"You must have heard the commotion as the guards were chasing me. I tripped and dropped the horn, but before the guards grabbed me, I hid one of the broken pieces in my pocket."

The servant snatches the horn from your hand. "I thought you were innocent! I can't believe someone so young would really steal the unicorn horn." He leaves your cell and locks the door, then spits on the ground. "You deserve death."

With each passing day your hunger and thirst become more overwhelming. You wait in your miserable cell, hoping a guard will bring you food and water, but no one comes. Your only visitor is death.

The End

You never know whether they understand your plea or if the terror of their entrapment makes the birds weep. You watch in astonishment as the first tiny tears glisten in the eyes of the hummingbirds. The swallows sob, and shiny teardrops slide down the long bills of the woodpeckers.

"It's working!" cries the unicorn over the noise of beating wings and the piercing cries of the birds.

A glorious rainbow arches from the moon to the earth. Slowly the unicorn's horn grows long and lustrous, glowing with a light of its own. When you finally release the birds from the golden net, they soar freely through the forest.

"I owe you my life," the unicorn tells you. "How can I repay you?"

You are so awed by the wonder of the evening that it takes you a moment to speak. "For me seeing the Rainbow of Tears has been enough, but my village needs your help."

"Take me there. I'll do whatever I can," replies the unicorn. The two of you turn toward the sunrise and walk to your village.

The End

You land smoothly and hop over to the unicorn. You try to say "Hi, it's me," but all that comes out are some unfamiliar chirps. When you turn to your fellow swallow, the sorceress, you spot a fox lunging into the clearing.

Before you can utter a single peep, the fox snatches the swallow-sorceress in its mouth and runs off. You watch, hoping the sorceress will quickly turn herself into a woman or the wind—or anything—but nothing happens.

You notice the vial of potion has fallen from the basket. No matter how hard you try, you can't pick it up with your beak. With sickening panic you realize the unicorn will die, and you will spend the rest of your life as a swallow.

The End

ABOUT THE AUTHOR

Deborah Lerme Goodman has a BFA in weaving and a graduate degree in museum education. She began writing for children as an education coordinator at the Smithsonian Institution, where her books *The Magic Shuttle* and *Bee Quilting* were published. Ms. Goodman has also written *The Throne of Zeus* in the Bantam Choose Your Own Adventure series, writes for several magazines, and invents games. She lives in Cambridge, Massachusetts, with her husband, John.

ABOUT THE ILLUSTRATOR

Ron Wing is a cartoonist and illustrator who has contributed work to many publications. For the past several years, he has illustrated the Bantam humor series, Larry Wilde's Official Joke Books. In addition, he has illustrated *Search for the Mountain Gorillas* and *The Throne of Zeus* in the Bantam Choose Your Own Adventure series. A graduate of Pratt Institute, he now lives and works in Benton, Pennsylvania, where he pursues his love of painting.